To: Hailey
Remember ya
loves you!
From: Tonya M. Berg
10-6-13

Maynard
the Teddy Bear

by Ms. Tanya Bex

DORRANCE PUBLISHING CO., INC.
PITTSBURGH, PENNSYLVANIA 15222

Dorrance Publishing Co., Inc.
701 Smithfield Street
Pittsburgh, PA 15222
Visit our website at *www.dorrancebookstore.com*

ISBN: 978-1-4349-6964-4
eISBN: 978-1-4349-6884-5

Maynard
the Teddy Bear

Maynard the Teddy Bear

Beside a little brook, back in the forest, lives the little boy with his mother. Now, the little boy's teddy bear, Maynard, is much more than just an ordinary teddy bear. You see, he has been hand-made with love by the little boy's Nana. That, indeed, makes Maynard very, very special!

With a big red bow around Maynard's neck from her apron strings, his eyes the shiny black buttons of her winter overcoat, Maynard's nose and mouth are sewn into a smile that seems to be directed at him. Maynard's body is soft, cuddly, and looking handsome in his quilted green vest from Gramps' flannel shirt. Maynard has been handed to the little boy with an

overflowing heart on his birthday, and they have been together ever since!

One day in early spring, the little boy, happy to finally go out and play with his teddy bear, ever so gently picks Maynard up, cuddles him, and says, "C'mon, Maynard, let's go for a walk." So the little boy, smiling happily, opens the door to begin their morning adventure. Clinging tightly to Maynard, the little boy walks with a skip in his step. The air is crisp, and the dew on the grass is sparkling brightly in the morning sun as he heads for his favorite path. They walk through the trees toward the field where the grass is soft and warm with the morning sun. He sits down with his back against a tree at the edge of the field, and he whispers to Maynard, "Now, let's watch and wait for the magic to begin!" He smiles as he gives Maynard a soft cuddle, and then sits him gently on the soft grass.

Pretty soon the squirrels begin chattering to each other, curious about the figures next to the tree. The little boy giggles at their sound. Soon the curious bunnies come out to see what is going on, and they cautiously hop toward Maynard and the little boy with their noses and whiskers flicking in the air. Just

then a mother deer and her fawn step out of the trees, with their ears twitching, and carefully take a step toward the little boy as the bunnies sit at Maynard's side.

The little boy smiles at the bunnies and watch the deer cross the field, munching on the grass as they walk. Then, to the little boy's wonderment, at the tree line, there sits a cinnamon blonde bear with her cub! When the bunnies begin to play in the grass, the deer approach the little boy. The mother deer smells at Maynard and nuzzles the little boy's fingers. He giggles as he looks at the fawn, which begins to prance and play with the bunnies.

The mother bear would not get too close, but gives her cub a gentle nudge that it is all right to play. So the little boy, Maynard, and both mothers watch the cub, fawn, and bunnies frolic and play in the grass well into the afternoon. When the animals begin to leave, the little boy whispers to Maynard, "That was almost as special as you!"

The little boy got up and begins walking home because his tummy begins to make noises. He says to Maynard, "Thank you for sharing this special day with me." He holds Maynard close as he steps into his home.

The little boy smells something yummy in the kitchen and goes to explore it with Maynard in his arms. There by the stove is his mother cooking supper. She turns and asks the little boy, "Hello, son, are you hungry? Would you like some nice supper to eat?"

To which the little boy answers with a glint in his eye, "Oh, yes, please!" He places Maynard in the chair at the table and climbs into the chair next to him.

His mother watches with pride as her son eats all of his supper. Then she notices him yawn and asks, "Are you sleepy?" He nods as she picks Maynard up. She takes her son's hand and they walk up the stairs together. She helps him into bed and tucks Maynard next to the little boy.

"Would you like a story?" she asks. The little boy nods and holds Maynard closer to him as she begins, "Beside a little brook, back in the forest, lives the little boy with his mother…."

Maynard the Teddy Bear's Special Day!

The little boy awoke with the sun shining brightly. Blinking and rubbing the night from his eyes, the little boy sees Maynard and says, "Good morning, Maynard!" beaming at the teddy bear and giving him a huge squeeze.

"I have a feeling today's going to be a special day!" the little boy exclaims, jumping out of bed and rushing to get dressed. He picks Maynard up carefully and starts downstairs to get breakfast.

The little boy's mother, putting his waffles on a plate with butter and syrup, turns and kisses the little boy on the cheek.

And as he sits Maynard gently in the chair next to him, he says, "It smells wonderful, Mother!"

She smiles and says, "Thank you, sweetheart." She places a glass of milk and the waffles on the table and sits to watch him eat while she finishes her after-breakfast tea. He hurriedly eats his breakfast, anxious to begin his adventure with Maynard in the wonderful morning sun.

When the little boy finishes, he quickly picks Maynard up and opens the door to their day of adventure. He steps out into the warm early morning sun. Smiling brightly at his teddy bear, the little boy gently settles Maynard on the lawn chair underneath the big umbrella then turns and hops across the lawn over to the sandbox and picks up a blue ball.

"Watch me, Maynard," he calls out, knowing that Maynard will watch. He smiles, dropping the ball in front of him and kicking it, sending the ball flying into the bright sunlight. He giggles as he kicks the ball and then runs after it time and time again, knowing that Maynard is watching him all the time like a true and trusted friend.

Then the little boy's mother walks outside with a tray filled with sandwiches and a glass of iced tea. Calling to the little boy, "Honey, time to eat," she requests he stop as she places the tray on the table. The little boy, picking his ball up and returning it back in the sandbox, exclaims, "Hey! Maynard watched me the whole time!"

The excitement in her son's eyes warms Maynard's heart. Oh, how Maynard loves being so special for the little boy! He remembers the smell of the little boy's waffles, cooked with love. Maynard watches with pride as the little boy and his mother eat lunch in the mid-afternoon sun. Every time the little boy looks at Maynard, the little boy's blue eyes sparkle in the sun with such happiness. When they finish, the mother picks up the glasses and gives the little boy a huge hug and a kiss on the cheek. She smiles and walks back into the house with the empty tray and glasses.

The little boy asks Maynard, "Would you like to see something else?" With the imagination only a little boy could have, he sneaks up on his sandbox, which is in the shade by this time. Slowly, he reaches in and pulls out a frog. The little boy gets up carefully and tenderly walks back to Maynard to show him the frog that lives in his sandbox.

"See? This is also a special friend. His name is Harry the Frog," the little boy says, lifting the frog just in front of Maynard's nose so that he could get a good look. The little boy then places Harry the Frog on the table and plays with him gently, petting him but with only one finger. They play with the frog until the sun starts to set in the sky.

Then Mother calls out to the little boy, "Sweetheart, it's time to come in."

He hollers back, "Okay, Mom!" So the little boy picks Harry up gently and places him back in his sandbox. Then the little boy gently picks Maynard up and walks into his home where his mother places a plate of spaghetti and a slice of bread with a glass of milk for his supper on the kitchen table. After they have been done eating, the little boy yawns again as the mother picks Maynard up and takes her son's hand, helping him up the stairs and tucking him into bed with Maynard close at his side.

"Would you like to hear a story?" she asks. The little boy

nods, hugging Maynard close to him. She begins, "The little

boy awoke with the sun shining brightly, blinking and rubbing

the night from his eyes...."

Maynard the Teddy Bear's Colorful Day

The morning sun shines into the little boy's room as he opens his eyes, stretches, and cuddles Maynard. "Good morning. How would you like to take a walk with me?" he asks as he is dressing, and he gently picks Maynard up to go downstairs for breakfast.

This morning, his mother has made him scrambled eggs, bacon, and toast with a glass of orange juice. She drinks her tea while she watches the little boy eat. When he finishes, he puts Maynard's coat and hat on him and then puts on his own coat and hat. He then picks his special teddy bear up and opens the door for another day of adventure.

Once outside, the little boy whispers, "I have a secret to show you today, Maynard." He gives the teddy bear a special squeeze and sets out to begin their walk. "I found a new path, and it's really special." He steps gingerly over to the farthest point of his backyard. There, between two rose bushes, is a path hidden, yet still there.

The little boy tucks Maynard deep inside his coat, with just his furry nose and ears poking out so that Maynard can see, yet protecting his fur from getting any snags by the branches. He crawls past the rose bushes, slowly standing, and brushes himself off. He walks a path thick with the fallen colorful leaves that make a sound, crisp like the air.

The little boy kicks at the leaves as he walks on this new path. The leaves rustle in the air. There are red, gold, orange, and brown leaves, too! Maynard is pleasantly admiring all the colors as the path rounds a bend. "We're almost there, May-nard!" he state as he continues to kick the colorful leaves, show-ering the air with bright colors and a crisp sound. Just when Maynard thinks they have gone too far, the path opens to a

little patch of grass by a brook where the little boy sits and then places Maynard in his lap to keep him warm, safe, and clean.

Just before them comes a sound Maynard has never heard before. "That, my friend, is a little brook!" the little boy exclaims as his eyes dance in the sunlight. "Listen to the sound of the water. Can you hear it rumbling over the rocks?" The little boy fell silent to let Maynard hear as he sighs, "Don't you think it sounds peaceful? I think it's a wonderful sound."

Maynard and the little boy sit there for a long time, listening to the brook and looking at all the colors left in the trees, as if someone splashes a painting with all the colors of a rainbow. The leaves rustle their sound, making a song with the brook. Some leaves float silently to the ground as the crystal clear brook endlessly rumbles over the stones.

Just then, something wondrous appears, even a little startling! A small fish jumps out of the water and splashes as it lands on the other side of a stone, disappearing under the ripples. "Wow!" the little boy exclaims, as Maynard silently agrees. They sit there until almost sunset, hoping to

see another fish. As they listen to the brook and look at the leaves, the little boy states, "Time to go home, my friend." He gently picks his teddy bear up, places him back in his coat, and heads for home.

The little boy opens the door to a wondrous smell from the kitchen. He puts both his and Maynard's coats and hats away. He then walks into the kitchen as his mother places a bowl of homemade beef stew, buttered bread, and a glass of milk on the table.

"You are just in time! Are you hungry?" his mother asks.

"Oh, yes, I am!" he exclaims as he begins to eat supper with his mother.

When he finishes, he yawns again and picks Maynard up, as his mother takes his hand and helps him upstairs and tucks him into bed, placing Maynard close to him. "Would you like to hear a story?" she asks. He nods, cuddling Maynard closer.

The mother begins as she pulls the covers tighter under her son's chin. "The morning sun shines into the little boy's room as he opens his eyes, stretches, and cuddles Maynard...."

Maynard the Teddy Bear's First Cold Flakes

Although the morning is cloudy, the daylight wakens the little boy. He stretches and snuggles Maynard closer. His eyes flutter open, and he sits up and looks out the window. "Maynard, it's snowing! C'mon, let's go!" he exclaims, bouncing out of bed and excitedly getting dressed before putting Maynard's red sweater on.

The little boy holds tightly onto Maynard as he bounds downstairs to his breakfast. "Mother, can we go out and play today?" he asks as his mother places his warm oatmeal with peaches and cream, toast, and a glass of milk on the table.

"Of course, sweetheart, as long as you dress warm," she says, smiling down into the little boy's sparkling blue eyes.

"Oh, I promise!" he exclaims.

When he finishes, he puts his hat, coat, mittens, scarf, and boots on. Then the little boy dresses Maynard the same way. He opens the door to their next adventure.

The air is cold as the snowflakes are floating gently to the ground. The snow makes crunching noises under the little boy's boots. He walks around the front yard as a snowflake floats down onto Maynard's nose. It is cold, but it melts almost immediately. Seeing the melting snowflakes on Maynard, the little boy sits the teddy bear on the front porch swing that has a covering draping over it, protecting Maynard from the falling snow. The little boy smiles, feeling assured of Maynard's protection, and then turns to play in the first snow of the year.

"Watch me, Maynard!" the little boy calls, as he picks a scoop of new snow up into his bright green mittens, forming a ball. He throws the snowball at a tree, narrowly missing. "Darn, I'm gonna try that again." He frowns, disappointment

clearly showing with his first effort of the season. The little boy tries over and over again to hit the tree in the front yard. Finally, he hits the tree. The little boy smiles and tries again, hitting the tree in the center of its trunk. "Yeah! I knew that I could do it!" the little boy hollers with pride.

"Do you know what else we can do with this stuff?" he asks Maynard as he stops to gather more snow. Only this time, instead of throwing it at a tree, he begins rolling it in the snow, making the ball bigger and bigger. Then he starts another one and places the second smaller snowball on top of the first larger snowball. Finally, he begins a third snowball as his cheeks are getting rosy with the physical play. He places the third smaller ball on top of the other two, making a tower of three snowballs. The little boy then places his scarf and hat on his snowball tower. He breaks off a couple of branches, poking them on each side of the second ball of his tower of snowballs. Maynard, having no idea what the little boy has been doing, silently watches the little boy intently. Then the little boy gathers some stones to create a face with two eyes, a nose, and a

smile. "This is our new friend, Maynard!" he calls out to his special teddy bear. "What do you think we should name him?" he asks his friend as he comes up to sit on the front porch swing with Maynard. He sits, looking at the snowman for a long time, trying to think of the perfect name. "I got it," he states as he picks Maynard up to carry him to their new friend. "I think his name should be Sunny!" The little boy giggles as he dances around Sunny while holding Maynard tightly in his arms.

Just then the little boy's mother calls out to him, "Honey, would you like to come in for some hot cocoa?"

The little boy thinks for a moment. "That sounds great! I made a new friend!" the little boy says as he motions to Sunny the Snowman.

"So I see." She smiles at her son. The little boy then takes Maynard into the warm house for hot cocoa and supper, which is roast beef, mashed potatoes, and corn.

When the little boy finishes eating, he yawns. At that moment, his mother picks the little teddy bear up, takes her son's hand, and helps him upstairs and into bed. She then tucks Maynard in close.

"Would you like to hear a story?" she asks the little boy. He nods, pulling Maynard closer.

"Although the morning is cloudy, the daylight wakens the little boy. He stretches and snuggles Maynard closer...."